www.mascotbooks.com

The Stinky Day

For more information, please contact:
Mascot Books
620 Herndon Parkway #320
Herndon, VA 20170
info@mascotbooks.com

Library of Congress Control Number: 2018902080

CPSIA Code: PRT0518A
ISBN-13: 978-1-68401-766-9

Printed in the United States

A A C AND ME
MYSTERIES PRESENTS

Ashley

Aya

Camila

Bogale

Gracie

Cooper

THE
STINKY DAY

BY B. SOMER   ILLUSTRATED BY VALERIE BOUTHYETTE

It started with an early morning eye-opening whiff,

Followed by a sit-up-in-bed curiosity sniff.

Then an angry look at my brother in
the other bed,

Who denied it, and I believed him,
when he looked at me and said,

"You know I'm the stinkiest person at the school

And I always make the most bubbles in the summer at the pool."

"But as much as I would like to take responsibility,

This stink is way too much, way too much for even me!"

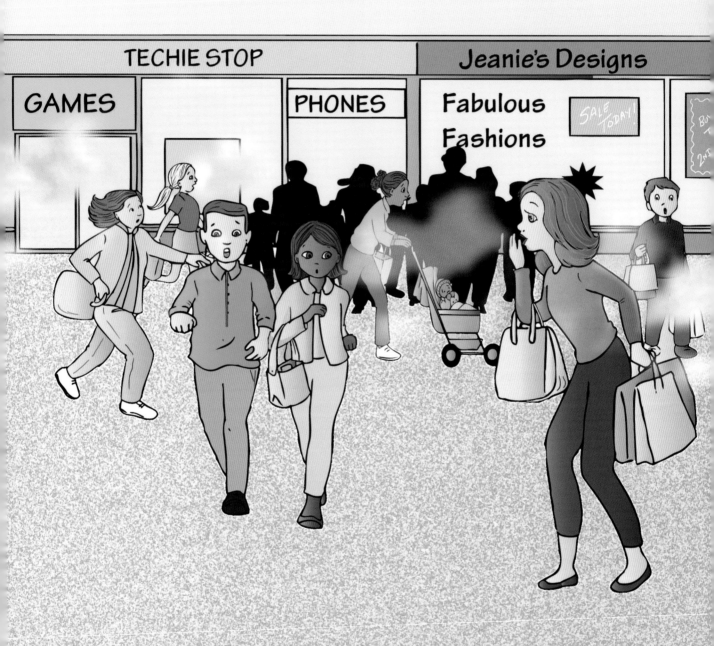

So I looked at our dog, but he shook his head *no way*

And the parrot in the corner didn't know what to say.

Next I went down the stairs to investigate.

Then outside, across the yard,
and through the gate.

As I walked down the street longer and longer,

The smell outside got stronger and stronger.

Seems everyone but me had stayed indoors.

No one was outside shopping at the stores.

They could have been buying one of these or those,

But it's hard to shop while holding your nose.

Then I walked back home and turned on the TV set.

The stink was still a mystery, they hadn't solved it yet.

Then I called Aya and Ashley to see

If they could find Camila and meet up with me.

Walking through my yard, Camila tripped on a hole

And the first thing she saw was the face of a mole.

And another, and another, and then two others.

Five all together and two who were brothers.

Then the two brothers, Marty and Maury,

Told everyone what happened and this is the story.

Milton wasn't like the other moles

Who spent the day just digging holes,

He always dreamed of fairy tales

And pirate ships with awesome sails.

One day when he was sailing on a tuna can,

He saw something interesting lying in the sand.

He jumped down and hurried over to investigate

Picked it up, turned it over, smelled it, and then ate.

His mouth got hot, his eyes got big, and smoke came out his ears.

Then he dug more tunnels than he had dug in years.

He dug under the whole town in every direction

And popped his head out of the ground at every intersection.

Through parts of town built long ago and some much newer,

Through rocks and dirt and junk and a pipe from the sewer.

The stink filled all the tunnels and came out of the ground.

It smelled up all the buildings and houses in the town.

So the city workers fixed the pipe crack.

When they were finished they put the dirt back.

Then everyone, including the moles,

Helped to fill in all of the holes.

We had a picnic out in the fresh air

With lots of sandwiches and cookies to share.

So AAC and me

Solved another mystery.

Don't miss our next adventure:

The Missing Chicken